LITTLE RED RHYMING HOOD

Sue Fliess   pictures by Petros Bouloubasis

Albert Whitman & Company
Chicago, Illinois

Once there was a girl who spoke only in rhyme. This drew some attention.

"Want to ride the swings with me?
Race our bikes or climb a tree?"

"Look, everybody, the sad little rhymer has no friends," teased Big Brad Wolf.

"You don't bother me, Big Brad.
Nasty words won't make me sad."

But his words did bother her.

One day after playing at the
park, she said to her grandma,

"I wish I was not this way.
May I hide in here today?"

To cheer her up, Grandma sewed
her a cozy, red, hooded sweatshirt.

"This new hoodie looks just right.
I shall wear it day and night!"

She wore it everywhere she
went. And so she became known
as Little Red Rhyming Hood.

Now every day after school, Little Red walked straight to Grandma's house. And every day, Brad Wolf tried to scare her.

"Boo!" boomed Brad.

"Gotcha, Little Red!"

"You couldn't scare me if you tried.
Stop it, Brad. Now step aside."

One afternoon, Grandma showed
Little Red a flyer for a poetry contest.

"Maybe I'll meet kids like me,
Who also speak in poetry!"

Little Red practiced each day while she walked. On the day of the contest, she was so focused on her poem that she didn't hear Brad sneak up behind her.

bush?"

For the first time ever, Red didn't rhyme.

"Yes! I really scared you good!

Now who's brave, Red Rhyming Hood?"

And for the first time ever, Brad did.

"Leaping limericks!" said Little Red. "You've scared the rhyme out of me…and into you…and the poetry contest is *tonight*!"

"Help me! Make it go away!
I don't want to rhyme all day."

"Maybe I'll help you," said Red, "but there's no time to fix this before the contest. So first, you need to help me win it."

"Red, I don't think I can wait—"

"Shhh, I need to concentrate..."

"Hey," said Brad, "we rhymed just then..."

"Holy haiku! Where's my pen?"

So the two wrote
a poem together.

At the contest, they got on stage and took turns saying each line. Red began:

"Once there was a girl named Red."

"Who spoke the verses in her head."

"A wolf named Brad thought this was strange."

"He teased her, though she could not change."

"He scared the rhyme from her to him!"

"Everything was looking grim."

"Red began to miss her verse."

"And causing that made Brad feel worse."

"Maybe they would make amends…"

"Could these enemies be friends?"

Then Brad and Red grabbed hands and took a bow.
The audience cheered and howled with delight.

The two new friends left with the winning trophy.

Brad was so excited, he gave Little Red a **BIG** hug.

To my husband, Kevin, who is a genius—SF

To Jason and Maya (my cats)—PB

Library of Congress Cataloging-in-Publication data is on file with the publisher.

Text copyright © 2019 by Sue Fliess
Illustrations copyright © 2019 by Albert Whitman & Company
Illustrations by Petros Bouloubasis
First published in the United States of America in 2019 by Albert Whitman & Company
ISBN 978-0-8075-4597-3 (hardcover)
ISBN 978-0-8075-4599-7 (ebook)

Printed in China
10 9 8 7 6 5 4 3 2 1 WKT 24 23 22 21 20 19

Design by Ellen Kokontis

For more information about Albert Whitman & Company,
visit our website at www.albertwhitman.com.

100 Years of Albert Whitman & Company
Celebrate with us in 2019!